Oh. Hello.

You're probably wondering what I'm doing here in the dark.

By myself. With all this stuff.

If you guessed that I tried to run away tonight, you're right. I did.

Why? Well, that's a long story.

I can tell you, if you'd like.

My name is Louie, by the way.

Or it was. Now they just call me . . .

For Stacey and Kahlua

Printed in Dongguan, Guangdong, China.
Candlewick Press, 99 Dover Street, Somerville, Massachusetts 02144. visit us at www.candlewick.com.

TLF 22 21 20 19 18 17
10 9 8 7 6 5 4 3 2 1

MIX
Paper from
responsible sources
FSC
www.fsc.org
FSC® C104723

Poor Louie

Tony Fucile

CANDLEWICK PRESS

My life was great!

Every morning started with a walk,

rain

or shine.

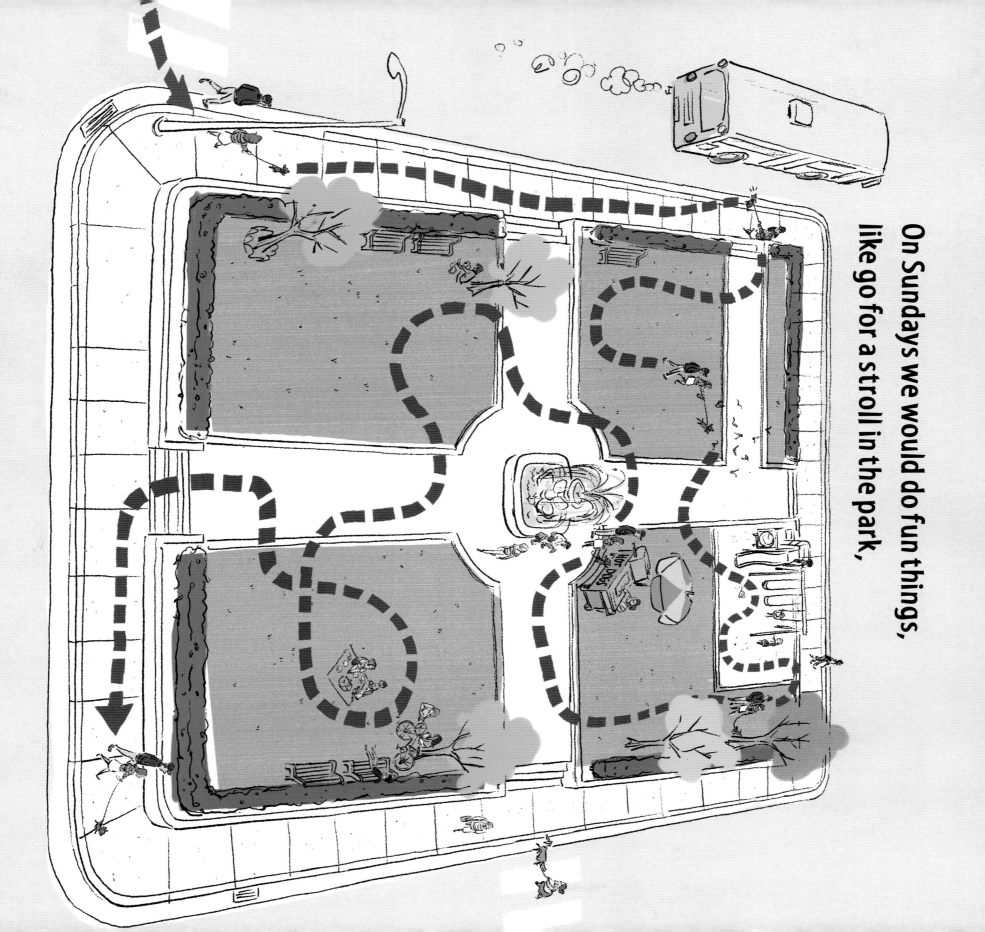

On Sundays we would do fun things,
like go for a stroll in the park,

eat ice cream,

or go shopping.

Pretty much every day of the week ended the same way:

dinner,

a movie,

a kiss good night,

and then off we went to sleep.

Once in a while, Mom and I would have a playdate with her friends.
It was great!
Everyone paid attention to me.
But then, one day, *they* started to appear.

First there was just one . . .

then two . . .

then four . . .

They pulled on my ears
and squeezed my tummy.

MOM!!

"Poor Louie!"

Yeah, I know . . . they smell good. And they do walk on all fours, I'll give them that. But JEEZ! All I could say was thank goodness we'd never have one of those in OUR house.

Yep, life was pretty perfect with just the three of us.

Then, let me tell you — things got weird.

First it was dinner.

Cold.

On the floor.

"Poor Louie."

I still had my walks, I guess.
Sort of.

Bedtime wasn't fun at all anymore.

"Pablo
Packard
Patrick
Paul
Peabody
Percival
Peter
Peyton . . ."

"Packard!"

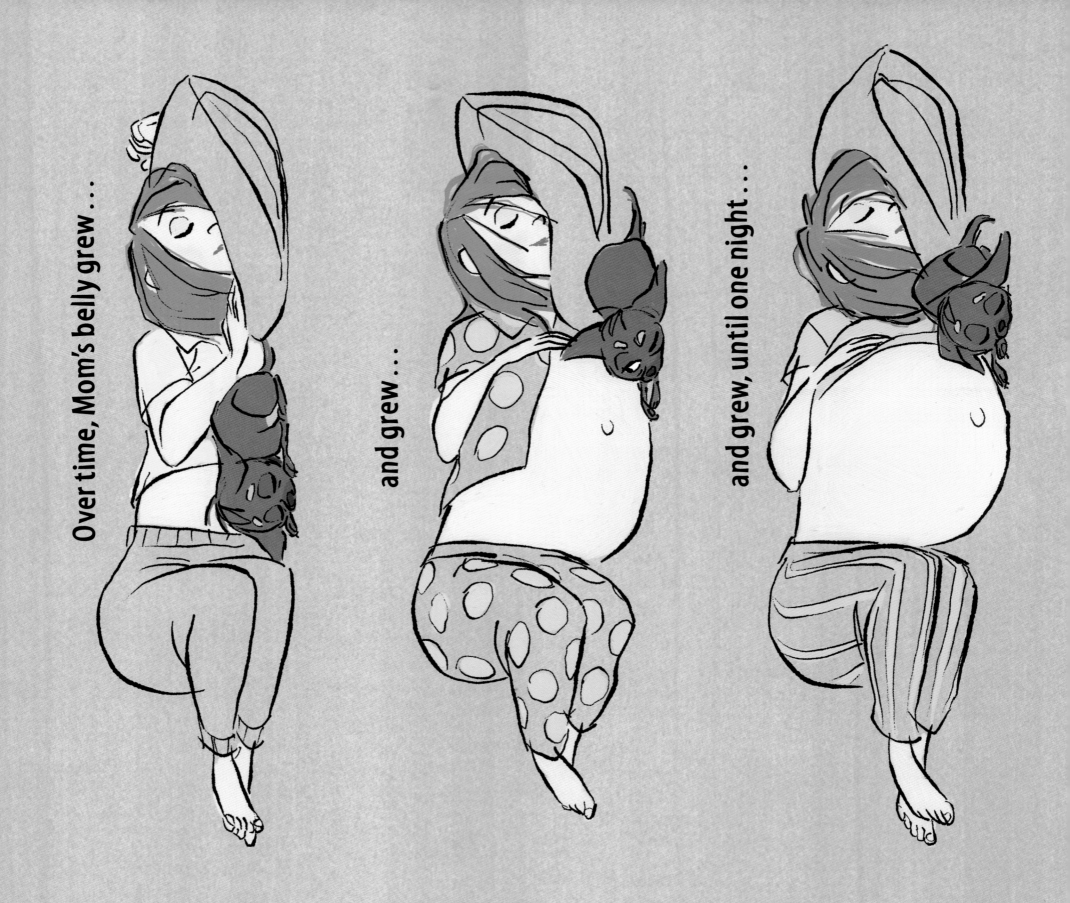

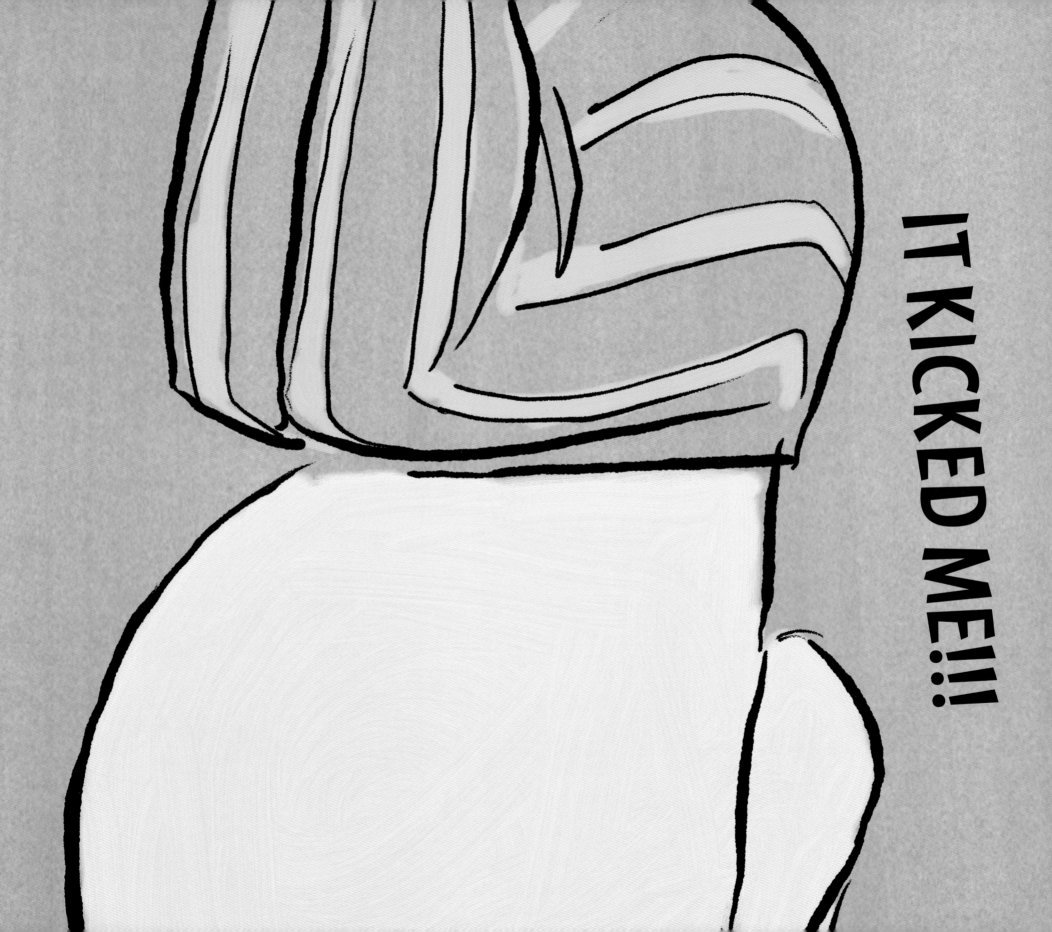

From that night on, I slept on the floor.
Just me and my food dish.
Things couldn't possibly get worse, right?

WRONG!

One day, Mom and Dad came home with lots of new stuff.

At first it seemed okay.

There were two beds. Fun.

Two hiking pouches.
Good, can't have enough of those.

Two sweaters. Cute.

Two hats. Okay.

But . . .

Wait a minute, I thought.

What's THAT thing?

Two seats?

And that's when it hit me.

One of those creatures I could handle. But two? No way.

Then Mom and Dad just rushed off and left me all alone. Not even a kiss good-bye!

Well, that was the last straw. I got all of my things together and ran away. Forever.

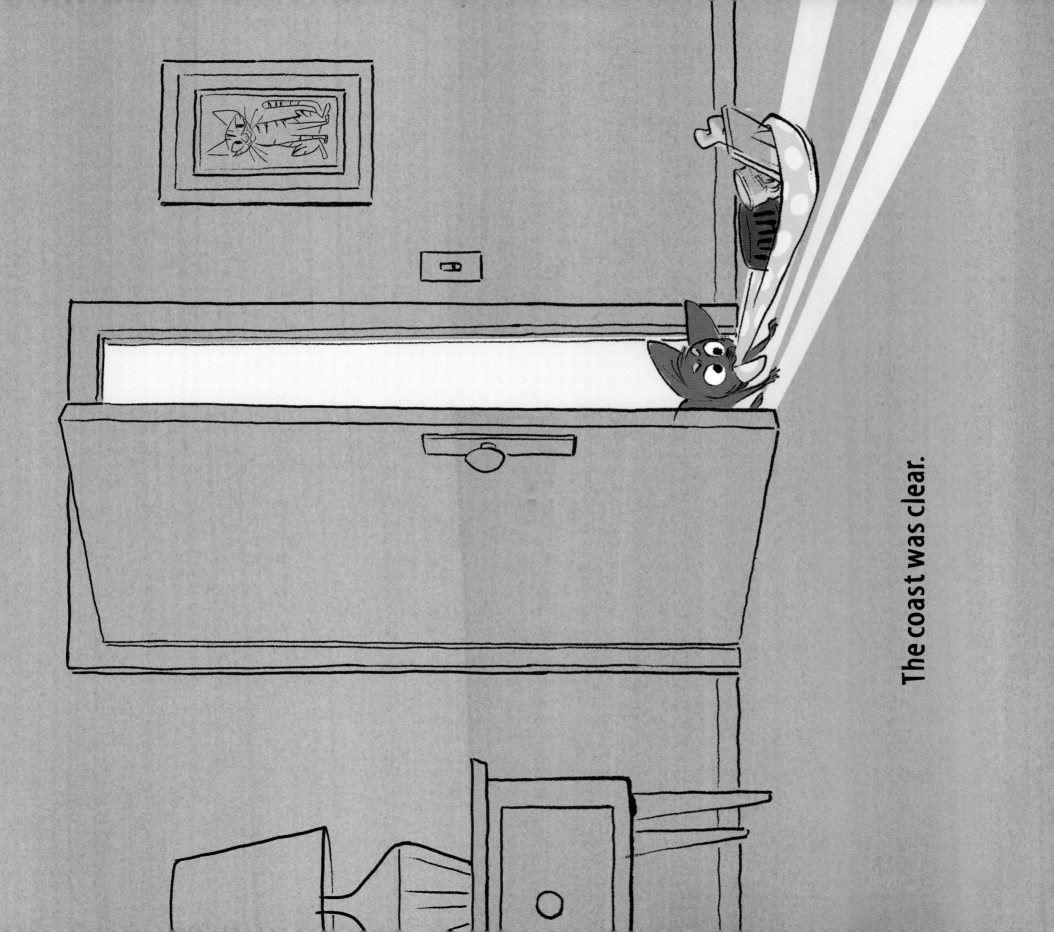

The coast was clear.

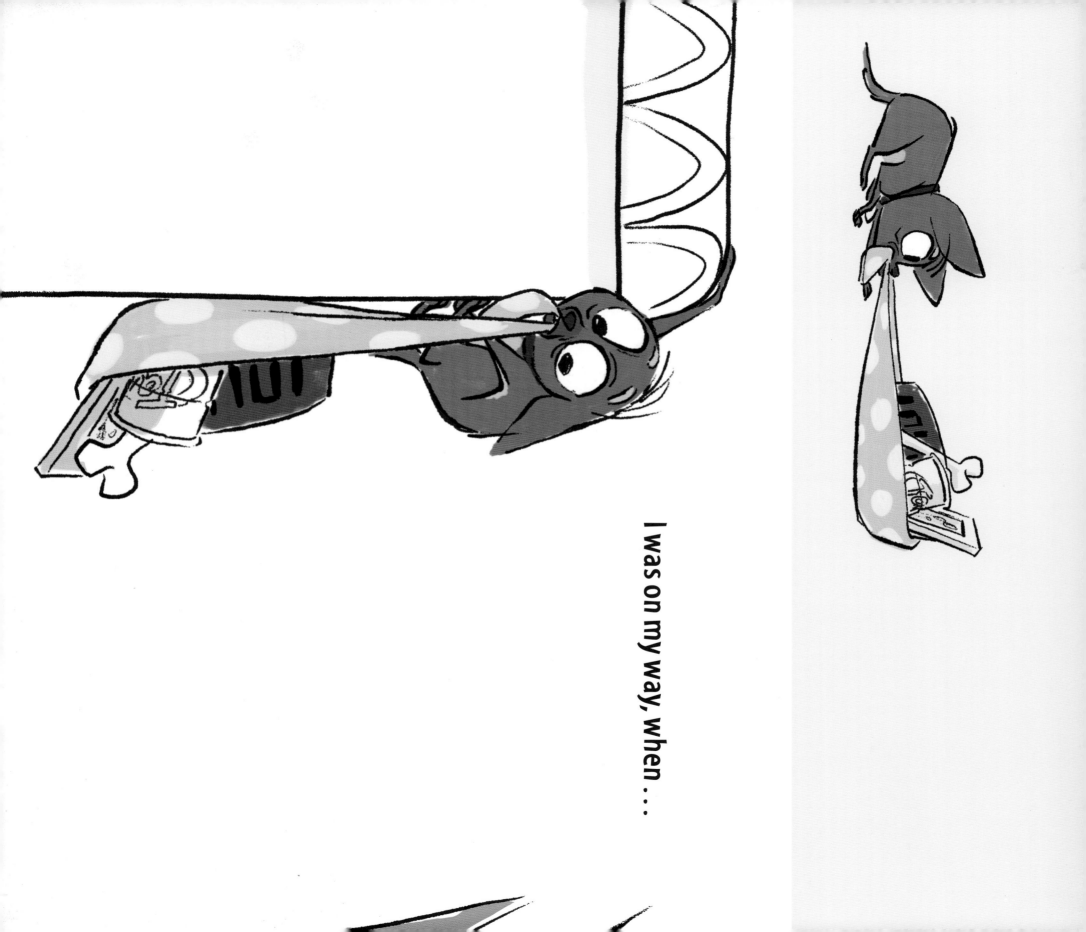

I was on my way, when . . .

"I must have left the door open.
Your mom and dad will be home soon.
Back you go!"

And that's it . . . . The end.
My life is over.
You can close the book now. Thanks for listening.

"Louie, meet your baby brother."

My baby brother . . .

MY BABY BROTHER!

"Poor Louie."